Ahoy!

Deborah Donna

SPLASH

THE STORY OF
FISH & SNAIL

Deborah Freedman

VIKING
An Imprint of Penguin Group (USA) Inc.

VIKING

Published by the Penguin Group

Penguin Young Readers Group, 345 Hudson Street, New York, New York 10014, U.S.A.

Penguin Group (Canada), 90 Eglinton Avenue East, Suite 700, Toronto, Ontario, Canada M4P 2Y3

(a division of Pearson Penguin Canada Inc.)

Penguin Books Ltd, Registered Offices: 80 Strand, London WC2R 0RL, England

First published in the United States of America by Viking, a division of Penguin Young Readers Group, 2013

1 2 3 4 5 6 7 8 9 10

LIBRARY OF CONGRESS CATALOGING-IN-PUBLICATION DATA

Freedman, Deborah (Deborah Jane), date–

The Story of Fish and Snail / by Deborah Freedman.   p. cm.

Summary: Every day, Snail waits for Fish to return and tell him a story
but their friendship is tested when Fish asks Snail to take a leap out
of their book to actually see a new pirate book in the library.

ISBN 978-0-670-78489-9 (hardcover)

[1. Books and reading—Fiction. 2. Friendship—Fiction.
3. Snails—Fiction. 4. Fishes—Fiction.] I. Title.

PZ7.F87276Sto 2013   [E]—dc23   2012030058

Manufactured in China

Set in Hadriano Std   Book design by Jim Hoover

ALWAYS LEARNING   PEARSON

*for Lucie, Emma,
Charlie, and Joe*

Every day . . .
Snail sits in one special spot, waiting
for Fish to come home with a story.

"Ahoy, Snail!
Guess what?
I found a **new** book!"

"A new book?
Does it have princesses, or kittens?
Will you tell me the story, Fish?"

"But I want to **show** you this time, Snail!"

"Fish, you know I don't want to go into other books. I like **this** book."

"Arrrgh, Snail, I promise we can come back here later. The new book has a whole ocean, and a secret treasure, and a pirate ship!"

"A pirate ship? Fish, I do not like to play big dogs, or monsters, or pirates. I want to play kittens and sleep right here."

"But, Snail! Sleeping cats are **boring**."

"Boring? Well, Fish, if you think I am so **blah**, and your new book is so **wow,** then maybe you would rather live there . . . with NO SNAIL."

"Well . . . maybe I would!
And maybe I'll go be a pirate by
myself and **never** come back!"

"Well, *fine*."

"*Fine*, Snail.
Good-bye.
THE END."

"But–

"that's not how this book is supposed to end.

How can this be **The Story of Fish & Snail**, with no . . .

"...Fish?"

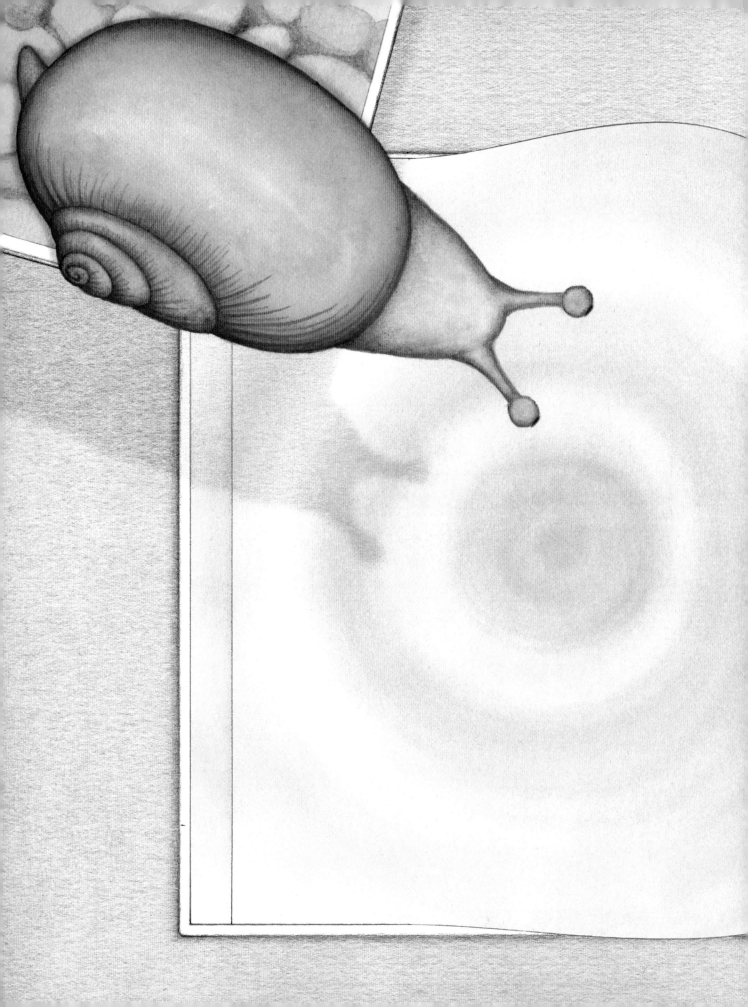

"Fish?"

"F-I-I-I-I-S-H!"

"Fish! . . .
Where are you?"

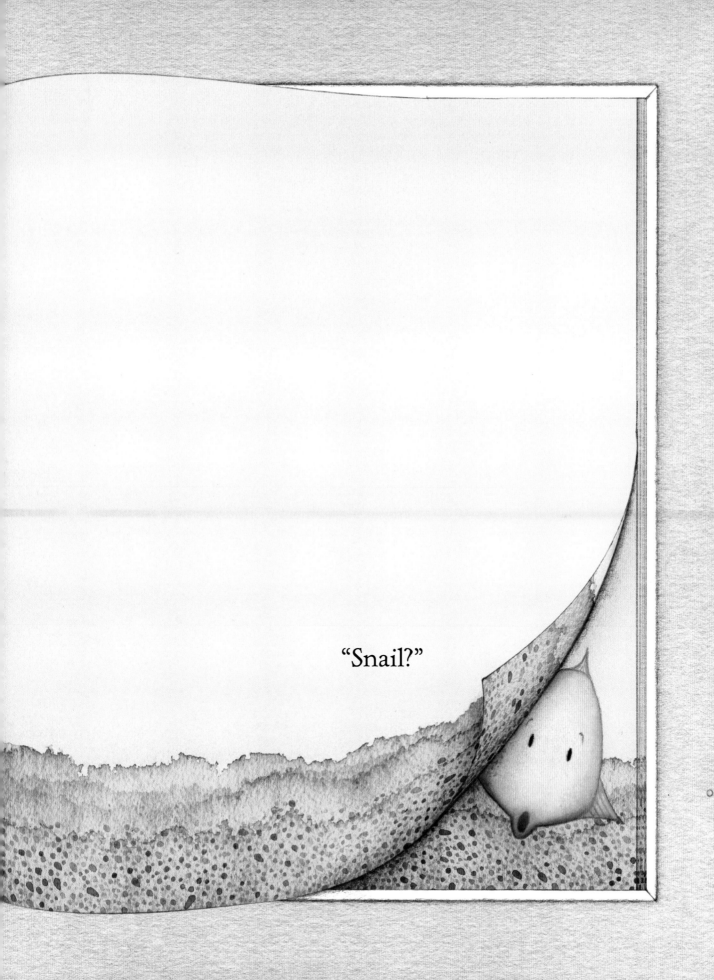

"Snail?"

"Snail, you *came!* You are very brave."

"Brave enough to be a pirate?"

"Of course! Or maybe . . ."

"What, Fish?"

"A *kitty*-pirate."

Together again, the friends set sail—
Jolly Pirate Fish, and First-Cat-Mate Snail.